for
Lakeside
Library

Donated by

Molly Canfield
March 17, 2000

To Pat Gauch, a true original
                              —J. Y.

For Kathleen and Neil Walsh, Brooklyn originals
                              —T. L.

The Originals

JANE YOLEN

illustrated by TED LEWIN

7386

Philomel Books   New York

Picture this: small leather arks,
waves lapping their sides,
and unsung Noahs at the oars.
In the boats, unsteady, stand
sow and boar, dark and hairy;
long wooled ewes large with lambs;
a pair of horned cows;
three goats, bearded, bouncy;
a rooster, red and nearly wild.

Who were these beasts,
now almost forgotten?
Ferried by many such boats,
scattered, like chaff,
from coast to coast;
shepherded across bridges
made of land.
And some remaining
in the great green pastures,
the stone-sown deserts,
the upland meadows, mountains,
of their very first homes.

The fair copies of these
fill our farmyards and fields;
refined, refinished, reworked,
reflected, reprinted, recast,
carrying but a small sketch of the years
printed in their hair, their hides.

But some—
ah! some are the Originals,
retaining a strong touch
of that first beauty,
their history written strong
in bone and skin,
in hoof and horn,
and the long, long memory of genes.

HEAVY HORSES

*Bred in the eleventh
century to carry knights
in armor, they now pull
heavy loads.*

Great-footed,
feather-footed,
iron-shod
gentle giants:
Clydesdale,
Belgian,
Shire,
Percheron,
Punch.
You tower over
those dawn horses
from whom all horses come,
whose small feet,
light feet,
bare feet
carried them swiftly
over Asia's great
and trackless plains.

CHURRO SHEEP

Navajo people still weave rugs
from the wool of the churro.

How joyous is his bleat,
The dark-faced sheep.

How joyous is his bleat,
Whose wool has two strands.

How joyous is his bleat,
Whose horns grow high and low.

How joyous is his bleat,
Whose wool makes my blankets.

How joyous is his bleat
As he grazes by my hogan,
Looking out into the desert
In the morning, in the evening.

TAMWORTH
A dark-coated medieval pig that never sunburns.

Oh, dark queen pig, the red of sun,
Who through old woodlots once did run
To find among the wilding swine
A partner with whom you could dine
On acorns, beechnuts brown and small,
You do not fatten well
At all.

This last might seem a detriment
To eaters lacking sentiment.
But oh—the lifeline of a queen
Who keeps her piggy figure lean.

HIGHLAND CATTLE

Found in Scotland foraging along
sea lochs from the Iron Age on.

By the black-glass loch
the young laird walks.
Cattle in his fields
Watch his passing.
They are all the colors of his plaid:
red and yellow,
black and brindle,
silver and white,
their coats thick as his own weave.
Oh, they are a fine match
for their young master,
shaggy and smart,
with horns of good length,
tipped with black,
like blood on a blade after battle.

SOAY SHEEP

The oldest domestic sheep,
introduced into Britain in 4000 B.C.

Over the moonface cliffs of Soay
small dark sheep are running
like brown shuttles across a weaver's loom.
Rocks and thorns pluck wool from their backs,
spinning it into sweaters for gulls.
Oh—do not smile at such fancies.
Even early man could weave dreams.

RED JUNGLE FOWL

In the Asian woodlands live
the elegant ancestors of all domestic fowl.

You would strut, too,
If you knew all chickens
Were your children.

16

HEBRIDEAN SHEEP

Sheep brought over by Viking raiders
who colonized Scottish islands.

Over the seas come the Viking raiders,

Horned helmets catching the sun.

Run, run, run

Into your *brochs*, hide behind the stone,

Take inside all that you own

To escape the fierce invaders.

What do they leave behind,
These raiders from the sea?
Scorched earth, a lake of blood,
The men who fought them dead in mud;
And strange sheep, helmeted with horn,
Graying with age, though dark when born,
Living wild behind the sea wall and free.

ONAGER

The wild ass mentioned in the Bible,
it travels the dry Asian Plains.

Freedom rides the desert wind:
You never knew the yoke, the reins.
But fetterless and masterless,
you track across the arid plains.

Among the cobbles, city streets
your cousins carry coal and clay.
But far beyond the city walls
you laugh the wind, you ride the day.

GOLDEN GUERNSEY GOAT

Ships sailing the Mediterranean
in the Middle Ages traded these goats.

The rich man's pet,
The poor man's cow,
A golden breed
From Guernsey now
From foul extinction's
Brink reclaimed
And by its island home
Renamed.

The poor man's cow,
The rich man's pet,
As pretty as
A goat can get;
With golden skin
And silky hair,
Although the breed
Is still quite rare.

WHITE PARK CATTLE

The white park cattle are the same
as those mentioned in the 12th century
epic poems about the Irish hero Cuchullain.

In the time of Cuchullain the Brave,

Great white cows

The color of milk, of whey, of snow

Grazed the green fields,

Horns catching the sun.

Many were the black-eyed, black nosed cows

That ate the grass of Cuchullain's land.

But many more were the battles fought

In the stealing of those cows.

And what of the brown bull of Cualigne,
Who could shelter a hundred warriors
From the heat, from the cold?
And what of the brown bull of Cualigne,
Who could father fifty calves in a day?
And what of the brown bull of Cualigne,
Who carried his slaughtered foe
In torn fragments about his brow?
Where is he now, that brown bull?
Dead of a broken heart,
Dead with a heart of black stone blood,
While the white cows still graze
Lonely in the green parks,
Quiet in the green parks,
Unstolen in the green parks,
Dreaming of the glory days.

GLOUCESTER OLD SPOT

A pig popular in the seventeenth century,
often fattened on windfall fruit.

Under tangled apple limbs,
Facing into autumn's grief,
Fattening on pulp and rind
Of apple windfalls, fruit and leaf;

Belly ripening with the fall,
Apple hard and apple sweet,
Gloucester Old Spot dined all day,
Fermenting into cider-meat.

LONGHORN CATTLE

*Cattle portrayed on Stone Age cave walls
may be longhorn ancestors.*

1879, The Caves at Altamira
On the property of Don Marcelino de Sautuola

Did Don Marcelino know—
When his candle picked out
Ancient dancing bulls on the cave wall,
Wide horns dead white
In the flickering light—

Children of that bull's children
Had gone placid in the green fields
Across the seas,
Safe from hunters and their magic,
Safe from the shaman's power?
In that hour,
Could Don Marcelino know?

EXMOOR PONY

Wild ponies that roam the foggy
moors of southwest England
as in prehistoric times.

The mist lifts on the moor
Like a curtain.
In the sudden downpour
All that is certain
Is one small pony in the rain,
Its mealy muzzle
Firm down in the grass
While moor winds puzzle
Its mine-black mane.

This could be today—
Or a thousand years past.

NOTES ABOUT *THE ORIGINALS*

Page 7   HEAVY HORSES were first selectively bred in the eleventh century in the Low Countries to carry knights in armor into battle. But when cows began to be used for milk instead of pulling ploughs, the big horses were used for that as well. In fact, heavy horses were the mainstay of farms until the 1940s, when the tractor replaced them. Such horses as the British Shire, the Scottish Clydesdale, the British Suffolk Punch, the French Percheron, and the Belgian—the direct modern descendant of the great knight's battle horse—are the best known of the heavy horse breeds. "Dawn horse" is what scientists familiarly call the tiny horses from prehistoric times.

Page 8   CHURRO SHEEP, the breed with two-textured wool the Navajo or Diné people use to make their famous rugs and blankets, were first introduced to the desert peoples of the American Southwest in the 1520s by Spanish settlers. In the 1860s, the U.S. army almost wiped out the sheep during their war upon the Navajo Nation. This poem is patterned after an Arizona Navajo song-prayer for horses.

Page 10   TAMWORTH, the most primitive of British pigs, looks a great deal like the pigs raised by medieval swineherds. The Tamworth fell out of favor in the nineteenth century because it did not fatten well. But with its dark coat, it is a good pig for hot countries because it does not get sunburned.

Page 13   The familiar long-horned, shaggy-coated red HIGHLAND CATTLE beloved by tourists can be traced to the Iron Age, 550 B.C. They were the foundation of the cattle-droving trade. Hardy animals, they foraged along sea lochs or in the Scottish hill country until they were four or five years old. Then they were driven south to market, often forced to swim rivers or lochs on their way. Nowadays Highland cattle (or "koo") come in many different colors.

Page 15   SOAY SHEEP were probably introduced by prehistoric people into Britain around 4000 B.C. They are the oldest of domestic breeds, still found on the isolated St. Kilda islands off Scotland. They have short, hairy fleece that is plucked, rather than shorn.

Page 16   RED JUNGLE FOWL (Gallus gallus) live in northern India, Burma, southern Vietnam, the Malay peninsula, and neighboring islands. They can be found in forests, thickets, and bamboo jungles. All domestic fowl are their descendants.

Page 18   The dark HEBRIDEAN SHEEP, with their two and four horns, were typical of the sheep brought over by Viking raiders who colonized some of the Scottish islands. A *broch* is a round stone fort.

Page 20   ONAGER, cousin of the domestic donkey, is the Biblical wild ass. Found in northwest Iran to Turkestan, running over arid, semidesert plains, it is extremely hardy, existing on coarse, sparse vegetation.

Page 22   GOLDEN GUERNSEY GOATS came from a line of goats traded from Mediterranean ships during the Middle Ages. A number of these goats were left on the Island of Guernsey, hence their name. Threatened with extinction in World War II when the occupying Germans ate the last of the herd, the goats were saved by Miss Miriam Milbourn.

Page 24   WHITE PARK CATTLE are the ones mentioned by the pre-Christian Celts of Ireland in their great epic tales of cattle raids. These may also have been the sacrificial cattle of the Druids. Cuchillain was Ireland's greatest legendary hero.

Page 27   GLOUCESTER OLD SPOT was a cottager pig popular in the seventeenth century, and most often fattened on windfall fruit and kitchen waste. Legend has it that the pig's spots were actually bruises made by falling fruit. It is said that Old Spot meat tastes very cidery because of its diet.

Page 28   LONGHORN CATTLE look a great deal like the now-extinct Aurochs portrayed on the cave walls by Stone Age hunters. One of these cave paintings was first discovered by Don Marcelino de Sautuola on his property in Altamira in northern Spain. Today's Longhorns were first developed in seventeenth-century England. By the 1820s they were part of a regular scientific breeding program directed by Robert Bakewell with the help of Charles Darwin.

Page 30   The EXMOOR PONY, living wild in the bleak, fog-filled moors of southwestern England, is generally believed to be the closest living example of the Tarpan, the prehistoric horse of Asia and Europe brought to Britain by migrating Celts. Small in size (about 11 to 12.2 hands high) they are hardy and strong.

Special thanks to Dr. Sam Ross, Green Chimney Farm and Wildlife Conservation Center

Patricia Lee Gauch, Editor